Walt Disney's CLASSIC Peter Pan

Adapted by Eugene Bradley Coco
Illustrated by Ron Dias

A GOLDEN BOOK • NEW YORK
Western Publishing Company, Inc., Racine, Wisconsin 53404

There was a place, a faraway place, where the sun always shone, the sky was always blue, and no one ever grew old. This place was called Never Land, and it was where Peter Pan and Tinker Bell lived.

Not so very far away, in the city of London, lived John, Wendy, and Michael Darling. Every night they would gather in the nursery to hear Wendy tell wonderful tales of Peter Pan's adventures.

One night, when Wendy was telling John and Michael a favorite Peter Pan story, Nana, their Saint Bernard, started barking outside in the yard. Not a moment later Peter Pan appeared with Tinker Bell.

"I came to find my shadow," said Peter Pan. "Nana took it from me the other night as I was listening to your stories."

"Here it is," said Wendy. John and Michael looked on in amazement as she sewed it back onto Peter's body.

"I'm so glad we saw you tonight, Peter," Wendy said. "You see, tonight's my last night in the nursery, because tomorrow I have to grow up."

"But that means no more stories," cried Peter, "unless I take you all back to Never Land with me!"

Wendy, John, and Michael couldn't believe their ears. "That would be wonderful!" they all shouted.

Peter Pan sprinkled some of Tinker Bell's pixie dust over the children and told them to think happy thoughts.

"Now you can fly!" said Peter.

Suddenly they were all soaring through the skies of London, heading directly toward Never Land. It was the most beautiful place they had ever seen.

Down below they saw golden rainbows and blue waterfalls and mermaids singing in a lagoon. There were beaches and deep forests and, of course, there was the Indian camp! Yes, this indeed was Never Land.

"This way," called Peter Pan as Wendy, John, and
Michael landed in one of the forests. He led them to the
secret underground home where he lived with his good
friends the Lost Boys.

John and Michael played with the boys while Peter and
Wendy went to visit the beautiful mermaids in the lagoon.

It was there that Peter Pan spied the Indian chief's daughter, Tiger Lily, tied up in the boat of the evil Captain Hook.

Peter and Wendy could overhear the pirate demanding, "Tell me the hiding place of Peter Pan!" But Tiger Lily wouldn't tell.

"I have to save her," Peter told Wendy. They flew off
together to Skull Rock, where Captain Hook had taken
Tiger Lily.

There, Peter challenged Captain Hook to a thrilling
duel. Peter was so quick and brave that at last the nasty
pirate landed in the water, only to be chased back to his
ship by a ferocious crocodile. Peter rescued Tiger Lily and
returned her to her father, the chief.

Captain Hook was very angry. "That cursed Peter Pan! I shall have my revenge against him once and for all!" he cried.

He captured Tinker Bell and forced her to show him where Peter Pan lived. Then he caged her in a lantern!

As Captain Hook's band of pirates approached Peter Pan's home, the Darlings and the Lost Boys were coming up from the underground hiding place.

One by one they were captured and taken to the pirate ship.

"Peter Pan will save us," Wendy said bravely.

Captain Hook roared with wicked laughter. "Pan will never be able to save you," he shouted. "You will walk the plank!"

No one noticed that Tinker Bell had escaped from the lantern. She flew as fast as she could to alert Peter Pan.

Once Tinker Bell reached Peter Pan, he raced out to sea to rescue his friends. "I've come to stop you once and for all, Captain Hook!" cried Peter. "This time you've gone too far!"

After another fierce duel, Peter Pan threw Hook and all the pirates overboard. Hook was chased away by the crocodile, and nobody cared to save him!

"Thank you ever so much for rescuing us, Peter," said Wendy. "We would love to stay in Never Land a while longer, but it's getting late and I think it's time for us to leave." John and Michael nodded in agreement.

"Well, if that's the case," said Peter, "we sail tonight!"

Once again Peter Pan sprinkled Tinker Bell's pixie dust over everyone, and Captain Hook's pirate ship was suddenly sailing through the skies of Never Land, heading back to the Darlings' home in London.

But before Peter Pan and Tinker Bell started back
toward Never Land, they made Wendy, John, and Michael
promise never to forget them. And they never did!